Ekphrasis

Little Book of Myriad Stories

Dr. Guncha Gupta

Chennai • Bangalore

CLEVER FOX PUBLISHING
Chennai, India

Published by CLEVER FOX PUBLISHING 2024
Copyright © Dr. Guncha Gupta 2024

All Rights Reserved.
ISBN: 978-93-56485-81-5

This book has been published with all reasonable efforts taken to make the material error-free after the consent of the author. No part of this book shall be used, reproduced in any manner whatsoever without written permission from the author, except in the case of brief quotations embodied in critical articles and reviews.

The Author of this book is solely responsible and liable for its content including but not limited to the views, representations, descriptions, statements, information, opinions and references ["Content"]. The Content of this book shall not constitute or be construed or deemed to reflect the opinion or expression of the Publisher or Editor. Neither the Publisher nor Editor endorse or approve the Content of this book or guarantee the reliability, accuracy or completeness of the Content published herein and do not make any representations or warranties of any kind, express or implied, including but not limited to the implied warranties of merchantability, fitness for a particular purpose. The Publisher and Editor shall not be liable whatsoever for any errors, omissions, whether such errors or omissions result from negligence, accident, or any other cause or claims for loss or damages of any kind, including without limitation, indirect or consequential loss or damage arising out of use, inability to use, or about the reliability, accuracy or sufficiency of the information contained in this book.

TABLE OF CONTENTS

Acknowledgement .... *iv*

1. The Gift 1
2. The Blue Sapphire 7
3. The Lease 13
4. A Kind Act 21
5. Radio Romance! 25
6. Eau Calls 29
7. The Mourning! 33
8. Qurbani 43
9. The Fragile Mind 47
10. The Win 51
11. Manor House on Pennylane 55
12. The Runaway Mare! 69

ACKNOWLEDGEMENT

I would like to begin by expressing immense love, respect and gratitude for my father, Dr. Raj Naraina Gupta, without his constant guidance, I wouldn't have been able to reach this stage of publishing my first book ever. To him, I would like to dedicate this book.

This book is my tribute to my late grandmother, Mrs. Sushila Gupta, who was my constant childhood companion even in my naughtiest adventures and to whom I would sit reading out stories from primary to secondary school books and who would always shower me with choicest reactions of awe even when the same story was read out to her umpteenth time! She made sure I had a very happy and safe childhood.

To my loving mother, Mrs. Kanchan Gupta, whose understanding and unabating belief in my dreams has sustained me during the highs and lows of this journey. I haven't seen another as courageous a woman as her and it is from her I have learnt about perseverance and self-respect.

To my daughter, Myra, whose incessant enthusiasm and voracious appetite for my newest stories and poems infused in me such energy and vigour that I would be forced to sit down with my

Acknowledgement

laptop and begin weaving a new tale. Incidentally, she is also the illustrator for Ekphrasis. I am proud of her work and wish the readers will also relate better to my stories while seeing her work and find as much joy as I find every time I see the sketches.

I am indebted to my spouse, Mr. Nitin Navish Gupta, who stood like a rock in my difficult times of self-doubt. To him, I can only say, "I love you!"

I would also like to thank all the people who have touched my life, teaching me valuable life lessons through their actions that have been the foundation of my writing these stories.

Thank you!
Warmly,

Dr. Guncha Gupta

Story 1

THE GIFT

Sukriti dressed in a royal blue midi dress, lips painted, wearing a matching royal blue eyeliner, stepped out of her sprawling fenced bungalow, big loops dangling from her pierced ears, her high-heeled shining beige stilettos clacking on the concrete pavement. Tossing her head, her hair splashing around in a wave, she reached her parked car. Adjusting the side view mirror, she checked herself out before entering the car and putting the key in the ignition.

Nearby, the pullet from the coop in the veranda heard the clacking sound. Rhythmic music to its ears and immediately knew it would be Sukriti. It stared awestruck, its orange-yellow beak pressed hard against the coop net, admiring her like it had been doing since the past few weeks. Sukriti drove away in her blue sedan but the pullet, still immersed in its thoughts, strutted with its baby tail twirling like a frock. Unable to hear any sound, it seemed disappointed.

Mother hen quite aware of the infatuation but choosing to ignore, clucked - "Anna come. Have some seeds. Sony left them fresh, especially for you."

But Anna only had a mind for Sukriti and her high heels. She had taken a shine to those and there was no distracting it.

Every time Sukriti would step out, unknown to her, her high heels seemed to have a secret admirer in the little pullet. And the day finally dawned of which mother hen had been too afraid to even think.

That evening when Sukriti returned from her call centre job, shining in her finery, her feet elevated by a new pair of high heels, Anna demanded, "Mamma I want a pair of high heels." Now, mother hen was aware that her chick liked to watch Sukriti and might even be infatuated with the teenage girl but never in her wildest dreams had she dreamt that her baby's infatuation lay in Sukriti's high heels. Her first reaction was a humorous loud crackle. But then she looked at Anna and knew she had a real problem on her hands. Anna seemed lost, dissociated from reality.

Mother hen tried reasoning, "We are birds darling Anna. These heels, dresses and accessories are for humans. Not for us. Besides you are born naturally beautiful, my Angel."

Anna refused to listen.

Mother hen tried again, "How do you suppose your delicate feet will fit into those hard stilettos? And we live in a coop. Where will you go wearing those even if I were to get them for you?"

Anna seemed unhappy.

Consoling her, mother hen let it be, thinking it would get over the nonsense in a few weeks' time. But week after week passed with no alteration in Anna's behaviour on seeing Sukriti's heels.

The rooster was informed of the problem. He tried schooling the young chick. Crowing and clucking like a perfect coop inspector, the rooster scolded Anna. Anna seemed dejected. But when fall came, pushing out the stiflingly humid monsoon, as it always does, one day sometime after the midpoint of September, mother hen could no longer bear the sadness in little Anna's eyes. She resolved to find a solution and decided to venture out of the coop when the kitchen hand came to clean the cage.

Mother hen did a chicken dance as soon as she realised she had a solution. The next day was Anna's birthday and mother had an idea of a perfect gift for her little baby.

Early the next morning, as soon as the kitchen help came to open the coop to collect eggs and give it a sweep, mother prodded Anna out rather excitedly. Anna let mother show her the way. They walked to the old firepower, a dwarf bamboo shrub with lightly curled and textured fern-like leaves. The bamboo had fewer leaves growing from the culm than those fallen around it on the ground. And this is where mother gently nudged Anna. "Happy Birthday Anna!" Mother sang gently.

As soon as Anna's delicate claws touched the scarlet autumnal bamboo leaves, they rustled delightfully like layers of stiffened fabric. A clacking rhythmic soulful music of nature. Music like stilettos hitting concrete!

Anna was ecstatic!

She had her high heels!

She swirled and danced, clacking all around the ground as if playing note after note on an earthy piano. Her smile lighting up the ambience around her.

She'd received a perfect birthday gift.

Story 2

THE BLUE SAPPHIRE

Scene 1:

The scene unfolds in the Major's cabin within the Army Cantonment. Hawaldar Sukantu is seen preparing a tea tray on a side stool kept near the Major's table in the centre of the cabin. He put some biscuits on a quarter plate and turned to pass it to the Major.

"That's a Neelam, Saheb?" Hawaldar Sukantu looked admiringly at the Major's gold ring set with a shining blue sapphire, adorning the middle finger of his right hand.

"Yes Sukantu, that's a Neelam."

"Khoobsurat ratna hai Saheb." (It's a beautiful stone, Sir).

"Yes Sukantu, Amma insisted I wear it. Some astrologer recommended it to her after looking at my birth chart. Apparently, it can miraculously change the course of my life." The major chuckled.

Sukantu: "No. No Saheb! You must not laugh. Mataji is right (Sukantu left the kettle on the stool, looking up with a serious expression). This stone has magical powers. It is the stone of Lord Shani himself. No joking matter this. I do hope you've tested it first, Saheb."

Major: "No Sukantu I did not have the time to test it."

Sukantu: "Tsk! Tsk!

You should have Saheb. It is said that this blue piece of precious stone has so much energy that even if not worn by the user and kept nearby, like beneath one's pillow, it can irradiate and affect."

He is interrupted by the entry of Major's colleague.

Major Mann: "Come Major Singh! Have some tea ..."

Scene 2:

The night was dark and chilly. The moon was thin and crescentic, few lights lit the sparsely populated mountainous region far away from the cantonment. The Major with his colleague and a Hawaldar in an open jeep ventured out for routine patrolling. They drove uphill together for a little while. Upon reaching the third curve to the left of Kharoli Mountain, they split up. Major Mann alighted and ventured on, alone on foot, up the hill, towards the Kharoli plantation, torch in one hand and a radio walkie-talkie in his other. His sidearm was upholstered to the belt. His high boots making a light sound as he trod on the clearing along the hillside.

He must have walked around 6 km or so when he paused and turned his torch around, 360 degrees across the hill peering into the night like a cat on the prowl. Satisfied, he turned to walk on. His boots made a slight rustling sound and he stopped to examine the source, pointing his torch downwards towards his feet. Surprised, he picked up a long white unmarked paper envelope from the ground. He flipped it over and found a maroon-brown wax seal pasted across the flap, securing the envelope. The major looked around. He spotted no one. Pocketing the envelope, he trod along.

Some distance ahead, his mind still on the envelope, he decided to break open the seal, justifying himself in his mind that even if he had to report it in at the cantonment, it wouldn't matter much whether the envelope was open or closed. Besides how would anyone know who opened the seal? He could easily say, this was the state he'd found it in. Curiosity got the better of him and finding a secluded spot with an elevated milestone under a birch tree, he sat down to open the envelope.

The Major was a valiant man, executor of many a secret operation against ill conspiring men in the valley, in his past deployments and not easily excited. But he obviously was not prepared for what he found in the envelope. His torch slipped and his breathing could be heard loud in the pin-drop silence of the valley in the dark. Bending to retrieve his torch, he projected it once more towards the content of the envelope. "Just to be sure," he said to himself.

The white and sky-blue colour bearer cheque amounting to twenty lac rupees suddenly beamed like an amateur actor in the torch spotlight and this time the major corpsed like a supporting actor, reading out a real bad joke. The valley cracked with his laughter. And with tears flowing down his face, his mind started a dialogue.

"O mother dear! You were right, this blue stone did work wonders. My life is about to change! The Lord works in mysterious ways."

Then, a thought followed, "I wonder who this belonged to?" – (interesting how the human mind functions. The tense had already changed in his mind).

Unrestricted, a torrent of thoughts poured out like a deluge ...

"Am sure this belonged to a wealthy scoundrel, with no care in the world. God is just. He takes care of all His beings. I seem to be the chosen one!"

But thoughts, like rising curls of smoke, have a propensity to wander and creep unannounced. And not all of these, as experience directs, can take a direction all bad. For the major, like all of us, had a conscience.

"What if this belongs to a farmhand, borrowed may be from the landlord, for a child studying far from home? Or for an ailing child? For surgery?" Possibilities seemed endless (The tense changed once again).

His pace quickened as he turned back, walking towards the cantonment. It was late when he rang his superior's bell and handed over the envelope, making sure it was entered in the register and signed by him, his superior and the superior's wife as a witness, relief written all over his face.

Scene 3:

(Major's cabin)

Sukantu: Would you have your tea now, Saheb?

Major Mann nodded his head in affirmative.

Sukantu put the kettle on and started laying the plate of biscuits.

Major: "Sukantu. I have tested it."

"Saheb?" – Sukantu looked at the major, confused.

"The stone. Neelam. I have tested it. "The major continued.

"And?" - Sukantu enquired.

Major: "It suits me."

Sukantu: "That's very well saheb." (Sukantu beamed, proud of himself. He had convinced the major).

Major Mann turned the ring around in his finger thanking the Almighty to have bestowed him with good sense. Praying that the owner would approach the cantonment and claim what was rightfully his.

Story 3

THE LEASE

On a cold dark winter evening, a lone figure walked through a less travelled lane. A sinewy hilly passage with sparsely growing fir and fig trees, thinly covered with snow. The landscape as if painted primarily in black and white with a doodle of green paint made by a child on top of the existing canvas. There were brown, dead twigs from some of these trees lying on the ground. Air had a chill. Though cold and lacking colour, the valley had an attraction of its own. A perfect place for a writer, offering solitude and inspiration!

The figure was tall, medium built, wearing a long black coat and long boots, happily singing a small tune and enjoying a smoke as it trod on. Some wet grass twigs stuck to his boots like cat whiskers. The figure seemed to be in no great hurry to reach the destination. The juggling of the keys kept in his coat pocket occasionally interrupted the melodic tune that he sang.

The figure, as it turned, out was of a man in his late thirties walking with a purposeful gait, a pair of bright and happy black eyes, and a lock of black hair with few strands of grey sneaking surreptitiously – visible only to a keen observer! His nose was red from the cold and his hot breath colliding with the chill in the air made little curly clouds that amalgamated with the cigarette he smoked, the picture akin to a witch's emanating chimney. He would walk a little distance and then stop and gaze around absorbing everything around him, sometimes peering into windows of cozy little houses on the way, at other times staring into the distance. A few of these houses were candlelit, their windows decorated with pretty printed curtains. Orange rust flowers, growing from heavily spiked thorny stems in gardens in front of some houses, added a dab of colour to the chilly winter weather. The electricity seemed to be out, but candlelight and lanterns directed the man along his way.

As he walked further up, the trees grew denser and houses sparse. The man enjoyed his climb making up his mind to stay the night in case he liked the cottage he was about to visit. Suddenly, he felt a little tired. Up ahead, he saw his destination, a quaint little cottage with a dusty, faded red roof sloping gently. A dead chimney jutted out from the far-left corner and a shed covered the porch at the entrance. A low wooden fence surrounded the cottage with a worn-down gate hinged together with a padlock.

The dusk sun set, giving way to the moon and the sky turned a shade darker. The man waited, in no hurry, basking in his surroundings. He dropped the smoked cigarette butt on the ground, squashing it completely with his boot, before retrieving the key from his coat pocket and trying to fit it in the large, partly rusted wrought iron padlock. To his surprise, the lock gave way quite easily. He walked in. The calm and peace of the valley was momentarily disturbed by a lone fox howling somewhere in the distance followed by an angry chirp from some mother bird trying to make its chick sleep. Along the path from the entrance to the porch, weeds and wild plants emerged from the ground. The etiolated grass, that could be seen in the porch light, grew in patches with tan bald earth in between. The man did not pay much heed to these as he fumbled for another key in his hand.

His eye caught a movement to his right, and he noticed a large coir swing with dulled, breached coir threads hanging along a cobblestone pathway leading into an unkempt kitchen garden along that side. The swing swung in the breeze and the lamplight made pendulous shadows on the wall. Some fagged out vines crept lazily some distance up the cottage roof held together by tattered, faded ropes. There were two lamps hung on two trees on either side of the porch. Briefly he wondered about the lighted lamps but, was too excited to enter the cottage and was about to fit the second key into the main door lock observing its rugged flaky old polish when to his surprise the door opened from the inside.

A pale, fair old man with a long pointed nose, hooked at the tip, creases around the eyes, wrinkles on the face, loose skin sagging down at the mandible, his back drooping a little and a patch of pearly white hair stood in front of him; wearing no shirt but just a pair of loosely fitted pants. He was holding in his hand an old-fashioned kerosene lantern peering at his guest, eyes vacant, face stony, movements slow.

"Oh! Hello!" (A small pause punctuated by an embarrassed cough) "Mr. Victor did not mention anyone occupied this cottage. He said I could come up and look over the place by myself if I wanted to since he had some business in town." Here he paused looking on, prompting the old man to respond. The old man nodded his head, without a word motioned for the man to come in as he turned around, guided his way through a hallway to a living room. The dim light from the lantern cast eerie shadows as they reached a reasonably large room shaped like the letter 'L'. A dark brown suede sofa occupied the room and towards this the old man signalled the younger man to sit.

"I am extremely sorry," the man persisted, attempting a conversation. "I had no clue that someone would be here. My name is Roger Bond, and I am a writer. I have been looking for a tranquil place for inspiration for my next book. Mr. Victor suggested this valley and"... (his voice drifted as the old man turned slowly and walked out of the living room without responding).

Roger found this odd but was soon engrossed in observing his surroundings. The sofa he sat on was large, shaped like the room and occupied most of the space, its seats much discoloured, hand rests all worn down. A round wooden table occupied the centre of the room. It was covered by a thin white cloth like the drapes on the window, patterned with small blue and green flowers. An old stool stood at one side of the sofa with a porcelain angel, its halo partly broken and the white China within exposed. Its wings spread to catch attention. A portrait hung on the opposite wall. Its golden frame lustreless, almost appearing yellow and chipped off in places giving it an antique look from a distance.

His curiosity aroused, Roger was about to walk up to the portrait when his stride was broken by a pair of watchful green eyes peering at him and a black-orange furred old tomcat stole into the room, scrutinising him from top to bottom. Its gaze unblinking, the cat looked into Roger's eyes forcing him to re-trace his steps and reseat himself on the sofa. Satisfied, the tomcat made itself cozy under the lamp hanging from a rusted lamp holder on the wall above.

The old man returned with a tray. There was a teapot and a patterned old-fashioned porcelain cup and saucer. Aromatic vapours rose from the spout and the room was suddenly filled with a heady mixture of jasmine and hot water. Roger, all cold and jaded, welcomed the old man as he poured him a cup of tea. As he extended his arm, to hand Roger the cup and the saucer, Roger noticed an odd circular mark raised at the edges and depressed in the centre on the left arm of the old man. A peculiar dialect engraved in the middle. Roger took a sip of his tea mulling over the mark. Had the old man been branded? Or was it a tattoo? Should he ask him? Who was this man? Why hadn't Mr. Victor made any mention of him? Roger's head was spinning full of questions, but the old man had turned again to leave the room. Another sip and Roger felt a lightness in his mood. He relaxed on the sofa still sipping his jasmine tea. Slowly, he drifted into a happy colourful world of his own.

He was awakened by a soft thud and a purring. He saw the old cat sitting by his side as if to awaken him. Roger rubbed his eyes and looked around realising he must have fallen asleep right there on the sofa. Where was the old man? He got up to look for him. As he was about to go in pursuit, he saw the portrait on the wall. The background was dark, the scene drawn as nighttime with lamp light depicting an old man with a long, pointed nose, its tip hooked, few creases around his eyes, loose skin sagging down at the mandible, his back drooping a little and a patch of pearly white hair, wearing no shirt and just a pair of loosely fitted pants. Roger gasped and stepped back. Instinctively his eyes fell on the left arm. There it was! The odd circular scar mark raised at the edges and depressed in the centre with illegible dialect engraved in the middle. His eyes vacant, gaze stony!

Roger's head reeled.

His reverie was interrupted by a ringing phone. He looked around on the sofa and picked up his coat, searching for the phone in its pocket. It was Mr. Victor.

"Mr. Roger sir, good morning! How was your visit to the cottage last night? I hope it wasn't too difficult to locate. Did you like it? Would you like me to draw up a lease for you?"

"Aye! Mr. Victor, a very good morning to you too. Yes, I found the place alright. It is nice. The host was kind. I had a restful sleep after the soothing tea he graciously served me."

"The host? What host?" Mr. Victor's voice sounded strained from the other end of the phone.

"Oh! The fair old man from the portrait on the wall."

Mr. Victor was taken aback. His voice, lacking the earlier joviality, was replaced by fear!

Story 4

A KIND ACT

"These nasty birds. Look! They've ruined my little patio garden once again, pecking away at my lovely dahlias, scattering the basil seeds and my marigolds. Look at the devil's ivy. Oh my! Look at its leaves, they are all in tatters. These are a devil of the birds, I tell you," Mrs. Thomas was at it again, grumbling and cussing.

"Yesterday they soiled my clothes hanging on the line to dry. Today there are pigeon droppings all over the place," Her anguish was palpable in her voice.

Just then, the door to the balcony above Mrs. Thomas' screeched open and Mr. Joshi came out, water and millet seeds in hand, chanting a mantra he paid his respect to the Sun God. A flock of pigeons perched at various points in the community, waiting for their daily meal, immediately gathered, cooing and creating quite a ruckus. Their fluttering wings scattered millet seeds all over the place. Trickling bits fell on Mrs. Thomas's balcony.

She lost her cool. Yelling, she looked up, "What is wrong with you man? Encouraging these messy creatures. Come, clean my place too next time you want to feed them."

Mr. Joshi simply smiled. This banter was a routine for him, just as feeding these pigeons. A pious soul, he believed, he was doing what every human being should.

Now, Mrs. Thomas too, bless her soul! Was not a bad woman at all. Just that her rheumatoid-afflicted body could not take on so much additional work and these notorious birds did have a way of getting in her way. As if millet that fell on ground floor or in Mr. Joshi's balcony wasn't enough, they would find excuses to not just break their fast in Mrs. Thomas's balcony, but freshen up, passing night soil there too! The pesky feathered creatures liked to hear Mrs. Thomas's complaining voice, it seemed.

The entire morning routine kept the community entertained. Mrs. Gomes, the widow, would perch her rocking chair on the balcony right opposite every morning and would not leave any opportunity to record her observations on the subject, quite loudly too. "Tsk! Tsk! Pigeon droppings? once again? you say. But I do wonder why they visit your garden at all. I mean, we have a nice little bed of roses too, but the smart birds don't trouble us!" Rocking faster, she would egg Mrs. Thomas into a wilder frenzy, who would then take out her wrath on a nosey neighbourhood full of idle people.

Not to be put down easily, Mrs. Gomes would exclaim, "Oh! Do stop yelling. Be smart and plant some roses or cacti. Pigeons do get pricked too; you know."

Some days passed, and Mrs. Thomas noticed that no door would noisily open on the balcony above hers nowadays and no birds came to perch or feed on millet anymore. Curious, she looked up. Pin drop silence. She peeped down and to her surprise she saw a healthy crop of millet grass with yellow pearl kernels swaying merrily on the ground floor with a roost of pigeons enjoying their breakfast, cooing, fluttering and who knows maybe farting while they self-fertilised their prized land with droppings.

On enquiring Mrs. Thomas got to know Mr. Joshi had left for his heavenly abode. "Bless his soul. The man is taking care of these birds even after death!" Was Mrs. Thomas's last observation as she filled a mug of water and splashed it all over the little millet plantation.

The roost cooed happily, as if acknowledging her gesture. They left her in peace then on.

Story 5

RADIO ROMANCE!

Sujatha hurriedly finished her chores. Cooking, feeding Ammu and washing the dishes. Making sure, Ammu took her medicines and slept on time. 9:00 pm and power in the basti (slum) would be cut off. Sujatha lived in a rented one-room shack in the basti with her ailing mother and three-year-old son, Sudhir. During the day she worked as domestic help in the high rises near the basti.

At twenty-six, she was a widow. Sudhir was her life. Her husband, Parth had succumbed to Cholera two years ago and since then they were on their own. Destiny had not been too kind to her. And romance? Well, Parth loved her, and they were poor, but their romance wasn't. They had spent some loving times of togetherness till Parth was alive. Now? there simply was no place for anything more than work in her life.

Like clockwork, she would get up early in the morning, her day full of chores, all time lined and by the time she returned from work she would be dead tired. Ammu would sleep on a charpai next to her. Sudhir on the floor beside her, her arm serving as his pillow. Her old torn saree folded to make a bed sheet for the night.

She felt it first, a strange feeling like hair on the end of her neck standing up or a little tickle like a soft feather brushing up her neck and ear. Instinctively, she opened her eyes and saw a straight thin beam of light coming from across the street and falling on her temple. Before she could get up, a sweet burbling melody emanated from a radio pulling at her heartstrings. The soulful music brought a smile to her lips, and she felt fatigue leave her tired bones. She peered into the night trying to locate the source, but the light beam switched off. Listening meditatively, she slept peacefully that night. The morning rush made her forget the incident of the night…

Till another night descended and yet another song tuned into a frequency to match her heartbeat emanated from the radio across the street and the torchlight made sure that the trajectory was correctly mapped. Night upon night, the unspoken communication brought a yet unexplored dimension to Sujatha's world who, by now, had grown so used to the sound of music on the radio that any delay and she would start missing it. She took care of herself nowadays. An extra dab of lip colour, bindis that would match her saree. Little things to match the sound of music…

That night, the radio station was tuned in to play a special song. The dedication was made by a man named Ravi to the woman named Sujatha of Shakoor Basti - "Maana ki hum yaar nahin, Lo tai hai ki pyaar nahin, fir bhi nazrein na tum milana dil ka aitbaar nahin..."

Sujatha's heart skipped a beat. Could she dare dream once again? Could it be true? Could a humble radio conspire to bring two souls together? Did dreams come true?

Story 6

EAU CALLS

The grinding sound of a drill boring deep into concrete in the neighbouring house made her feel like her eardrums would pop out! Zoey, her daughter, out from shower, plugged in the hair dryer, Whirr, Whirr, Shooon... Whirr!

The noises seemed incessant. Triiii...ing, Triiii...ng... the telephone rang, "Hey Chelsea, I shall be late tonight. Please don't wait up," said Ralph.

"What was wrong with them all? They were too busy to give each other a thought. Love seemed lost." Irritated, Chelsea picked up her gear, deciding to go underwater diving, a hobby sure to lift her spirits up.

Deep Sea and around was a world far from being silent. The squeak of stridulating fishes, grinding damselfish's, 'Grunt! Grrrrunnt!', rushing Swoosh! of waves pulsing along the seashore, flock of seagulls rhythmically calling, Yeeeow! Yeee... Yeeee... Yeeeow! scuttling crabs in the sand, was all bliss.

Ekphrasis

A stork nosedived, Plorrk!, spattering water all around. Chelsea took a deep breath and did a back roll into the sea. Blotch!... Splash...sh sh...! Weightless, she relaxed, slowly adapting to the environment, blocking out the urban noises.

She reached the coral reef community, her preferred jukebox, Crunch! Crunch! Scrape! Grind! Crunch!... silence... Crunch! Crunch! parrotfishes chewing on coral heads and fluorescing reefs, an anodyne to frayed nerves. She basked in the glory of eau and its unique music.

Hours passed. Chelsea gave one last look of longing around and began to surface. She would've missed it, but the sound was distinctive. Squawk! Squawk! Squawk!... burst pulse-like echolocation emanating from a whirlpool. A light-bellied bull was circling around a birthing dolphin mother. A little tail peeped out of mother's underbelly. Rolling and pushing out, mother seemed amazingly calm during delivery. But the bull kept caressing her with his tail, rolling around her. The mother let out a single signature whistle! Phwwwwwhht! as if reassuring him.

Chelsea floated sanguine in the rhythm of the sea. Her eyes were transfixed. Reflecting on the time of her delivery, with episodes of bleeding and constant anxiety attacks. She remembered Ralph being by her side always, tender and caring, standing like a pillar. In that moment, she felt a sudden weight lift off her chest. Baby dolphin's body had by now started emerging and there was a pool of blood. The bull whistled and clicked, Fweeet, Tweeet, Tweeet, communicating reassurances, gently nudging the mother towards deeper waters, away from any lurking sharks.

Back home, "Bang! Bang! I was five n' he was six...," David Guetta's voice. Zoey peeked in, giving her a quick peck before retiring to her room. Ralph wasn't back, but everything seemed alright. Chelsea thought to herself - "Baggage of our expectations for appreciation and respect takes a toll on relationships. Rhythm of nature sets one free."

She was sleeping when Ralph planted a kiss on her lips. She smiled and rolled over...

——————— x ———————

Glossary:

Signature whistle: Communication through sound is very important in the lives of dolphins who emit high-pitched whistles. Some of these sounds are unique to each individual and are called "signature whistles," much like our own voices.

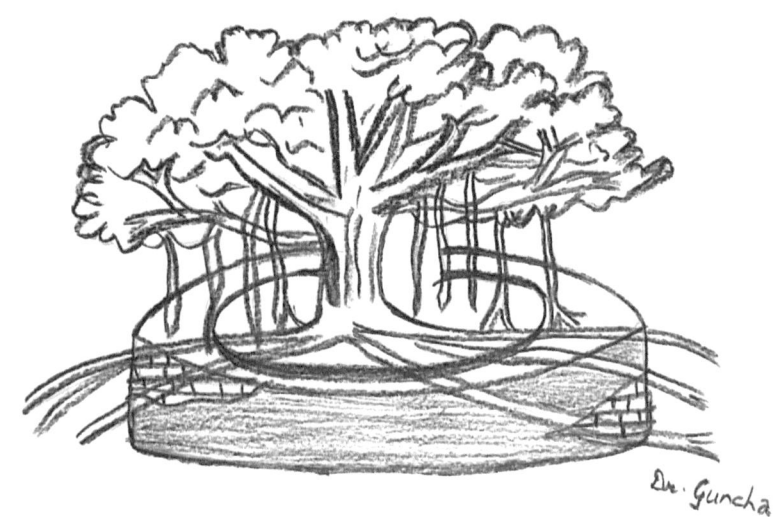

Story 7

THE MOURNING!

*I*t was a lazy hot summer day and the afternoon saw an intermittent stream of mourners gathering in the parlour of an old village house. Some coming in pairs, some in small groups of four and five, whispering in undertones.

The house was old and worn down. Wisdom of years gathered within its burnt brown brick walls. Wet dung cakes were plastered on the roof to keep out the heat. An earthen pot full of water stood on a tripod in the corner of the parlour. A long-handled steel scoop hanging by the chain on the side of the tripod for anyone who wished to quench their thirst.

The mourners left their footwear haphazardly strewn at the dusty entrance to the old parlour. The parlour faced an open courtyard inside. A sturdy rectangular pillar between the parlour and the courtyard created two entrance ways into the courtyard. An aged banyan tree stood tall in the centre of the courtyard. A concrete wall encircling the intertwined roots deeply embedded in the soil gave it a potted appearance and formed a circular podium for seating, a stage of sorts. The tree, mammoth, with old large leaves, offered a little respite from the scorching summer heat. Two dhoti-clad old men sat chatting in low tones on this stage under the tree. A lone jay bird looked forlornly trying to hide within a bunch of leaves. A tangle of sinewy sturdy long roots hung down like ariel anchors from the branches of the old banyan. A testimony to the wisdom the tree held, having witnessed multiple generations growing up, as did the prop roots, in its tender shade. Some brown, green leaves lay fallen around on the ground.

The air was hot and arid. Most people preferred the parlour to the courtyard. Inside there were three rooms aligned parallel to each other, with a kitchen along the left wall. All opening into the courtyard. A few women worked quite enthusiastically inside the kitchen, lighting the stove, filling water, passing the steel bucket full of milk, making tea for the guests. All the while chatting in hushed tones.

Today, the floor inside the parlour was neatly lined with two mattresses to sit on. Round pillows lined against the walls for anyone who cared to use them as a backrest. Old women sat on a few chairs in the front row, looking wisely on. A garland of yellow marigolds lined the neck in the photograph of Savitri Devi, displayed on a makeshift box covered with a white sheet against the rectangular pillar in the parlour. The room smelled of sweat mixed gentle aromatic fumes from the burning incense sticks jutting out of a ripe banana kept nearby on a stool. Prayer beads were kept wrapped up in a red pouch for the priest to chant, 'Om Namah Shivay!' A plate full of white and yellow flowers was displayed for the mourners who wished to pay their respects to the departed.

The Mourning!

A middle-aged man, his forehead creased in a frown, sat next to the framed photograph of his mother. Lost in thought, occasionally looking up to the old banyan tree in the courtyard in a secret sad camaraderie. The old banyan attested to young Savitri's entry into the house some thirty-five years ago, a lost and timid bride who took on the mantle of the household with grit, making sure that Amma and Baba passed away in peace. That Badi didi (Savitri's sister-in-law) got married in a traditional ceremony, as Amma would have wanted. When Savitri lost her husband to an accident, she became a mother and a father to their son, Samar. The old tree remembered the little boy Samar monkeying around, jumping and swinging from its robust hanging roots. It remembered when Samar broke his arm during one such antic and it remembered Savitri tearing at her saree to make a temporary sling for his arm.

Every time Samar peered through moist eyes, holding an unintelligible monologue with the old banyan, its branches seemed to droop a little. Occasionally someone would come and interrupt his reverie.

The old men sitting under the banyan tree discussed Savitri's life and her death.

First old man: "Good thing there was no pain."

Second old man: "Yes! She passed away in her sleep, they say."

First old man: "Pious soul! God calls only the good people to Him at a young age."

Another old man: (sitting next to Samar in the parlour) "Be brave son. It is all God's will. Do not despair."

Ekphrasis

Samar: "Yes chachaji."

Old man again: "Savitri was a pious woman. God shall take good care of her in heaven."

Samar: (wiping a lone tear that dared to fall on his cheek) "Yes chachaji."

Just then a dusty half inflated red, green ball came flying into the parlour and threatened to topple Savitri Devi's framed photograph on the ground. A small boy of four or five came running behind to claim his treasure.

A wise old woman on the chair saw this and called out, "Hey you boy! What are you doing here? Go outside. Go out and play. Where is your mother?"

A timid young woman, her head and face covered with her saree, ashamedly peered her head out a little to correctly identify her son and stood up. She silently cursed the little boy and clenched his arm hoping to deposit her bundle outside before other wise women could call out too!

Samar saw the scene and came to her rescue, calling out to the little boy.

Samar: "How are you son? Going to school? Hope you are studying well?"

Boy: "Yes sir!"

Samar: "Very good, very good."

Boy: "Is that Savitri auntie's photo? Where has she gone? Why have you put a garland on her photo?"

The Mourning!

Samar: (lost again) "Good! good!"

The wise old woman sitting on the chair cursed the mother who left a boy so young unchaperoned. The boy decided to run away with his ball even as the mother sunk behind some very accommodating young women pulling her saree down to make a veil. Another child wailed, hungry. The mother rushed to soothe him, lest she be the next one under the scanner, opening her lactating breast and hiding her baby in her bosom concealing it within the folds of her saree.

An old man sitting next to Samar nudged him gently trying to break this reverie. "Samar, how is your sweet shop?"

Samar: "Business is slow chachaji."

The old man: "Don't worry. All will be well."

A young wise fellow sitting nearby heard the conversation and said, "You must change the name of the shop."

The old man: "Why? What have you named it Samar?"

Young man: "Fresh sweet shop."

The old man: "What is wrong with that?"

The conversation suddenly sparked interest and another wise young fellow joined in.

Young man 2: "You are right brother. You should name it only 'Sweet Shop'. The sweets are fresh, so you are selling them. No need to mention fresh."

Young man 3: "Why Samar, you should consult a Vaastu expert. I am telling you, brother, these experts can change the fate lines in your palm. Did you not hear of how Karamveer's son, Kabir, failed his exams and just by consulting a Vaastu expert and changing a little layout of his study, Kabir did so well in his re-attempt."

Young man 1: "No, no brother, I meant numerologically. Jagan's uncle does numerology and see how good Jagan is doing. They change the name adding an extra 'w' to the sweet making it 'Swweet Shop' and it does wonders for business. It is an in thing nowadays. Haven't you heard of all these film stars changing their names and becoming overnight successes? It's all in the name brother!"

Samar simply nodded in agreement. Exactly what he was agreeing to was anybody's guess.

A man in a light green khadi kurta and pyjama came riding a bicycle and entered the parlour, leaving a mud trail on the white sheets. Silently he parked his cycle against the wall around the banyan tree in the courtyard. His hand brushed against the bell on the handle as he parked and the bell jingled mildly, disturbing the otherwise peaceful ambience. One of the dhoti-clad old men asked him, "Why could you have not left that thing outside?"

The man simply replied, "Last Sunday, I left my cycle outside the parlour of Jagan's house. While the Ganpati puja progressed, someone went away with it! This one I have borrowed from Kanti bhai. Can't really afford to lose another one. Savitri didi, well bless her soul (as he made a respectful mark of sorts across his chest with his hands) would not have minded, Chacha. Don't worry." And he went in to drink some water. He then went to meet Samar sitting still lost in his thoughts near Savitri's photograph.

Randomly some people would get up to go. Meeting Samar, consoling him one last time. Telling him how sorry they were. Others would come fill in the empty spots left by those who left. Samar drifted in and out of conscious conversation with people to his monologue with the old banyan tree.

An old woman with a crooked nose and pockmarked face gingerly got up, paused mid-way and nudged another woman sitting nearby to call her old man. She signalled to him receiving in return a stern stare.

Persistent in her effort, the woman made towards Samar. "Son, Savitri, Bless her soul, was a great woman, taking such good care of everybody. I can recall so many evenings having tea with her." Here she coughed a little, embarrassed, starting again. "Son! Savitri came to me a month back for a new recipe for special 'Rajbhog mithai' that you were to add in your sweet shop. And well she borrowed our iron wok for it. I was wondering if we could have it back. No! No! No hurry at all. Just wanted you to know. That's all!"

The fact that the woman in question was dead, held little significance as her life was finally summarised by these people in their whispers and undertones. That her life had been tragic and that she being a good woman would certainly find a place in heaven had been decided today by these mortals...

Everything was thought out well by these simple people. Little work left for St. Peter to do!

The irony being, that not even death can change much in people's lives. Life goes on and people go on with their petty interests and meaningless talks. And when everyone finally left the house, the true mourners remained rooted, one due to sadness and the other due to habit .... Samar and the old banyan tree!

Story 8

QURBANI

*I*smail, dressed in a new shiny green shalwar - kurta, excitedly pranced about the haveli. It was Eid-al-Adha, the festival of sacrifice. Mouth-watering food was being prepared and tantalizing aromas drifted from the kitchen into the courtyard, making Ismail's stomach growl with hunger.

Ismail! Ismail!

Rahim Qureshi called out from the main gate. Ismail ran out and hugged his father, demanding what gift he was getting this time. Rahim handed him a beautiful goat on a leash, its strong horns curvy, its jet-black silken skin, velvety to touch, its eyes sparkling. Ismail fell in love with it immediately. He cuddled it and stroked its ears playfully. The goat rubbed itself against Ismail's thigh returning his affection. Ismail dropped down on his knees, conversing fondly. A monologue started, "Oh! You are so soft to touch, so pretty. What must I name you."

When it was time, Rahim Qureshi asked his son to bring in the 'Qurbani' or the sacrificial goat. Ismail was taken aback. Aghast at the thought of parting with his newfound friend, Ismail asked, "What! sacrifice my friend? Why?"

Just then their neighbour, Rajaram Reddy entered the Qureshi courtyard with a box of sweets. "Eid Mubarak!, Rahim Saheb"

Hearing Ismail's question, he stooped down to affectionately shuffle his hair while answering, "Son, animal sacrifice or 'Bali' is an age-old custom, meant to please a deity; 'Shakti' in our case and 'Allah' in your religion."

Mr. Reddy had left. Unsatisfied, Ismail questioned again, and Rahim told him the story of Prophet Ibrahim who was willing to sacrifice his son at Allah's behest when asked to do so in his dream and Allah was so pleased with this ultimate sacrifice that mercifully He replaced his son with a Ram at the last moment.

"Abbu, I do not understand. So, Allah is pleased if we take someone's life and gift it to Him?" Ismail pondered for a moment. His face etched with perplexity and anguish. "Give me a good reason and I shall part with my goat," Ismail persisted.

"Qurbani means submitting completely to the will of God. It teaches us to share our food with all irrespective of caste, religion or creed. Also, we feed the poor on Eid. The goat is His creation. It does not belong to us, and we are simply giving it back to Him. We learn about the mercy of God, and we learn patience."

Ismail thought hard, not replying immediately. And then he said, "Abba, but give me a good reason, why we must take someone's life to learn these lessons. Reddy uncle comes to our house, we go to his, we share food anyway without sacrificing. You always help the poor even when it is not Eid. You have taught me that kindness is the greatest virtue. Then why don't you show kindness to this goat? Indeed, Allah is so merciful, why then would He ask for a life to be sacrificed when it is He who created it?"

Rahim Qureshi stared speechless. In Ismail's questions, he'd learnt some valuable lessons.

God is the creator of all lives. We have no right to take away a life that we cannot give back. And it does not take a sacrifice to learn life lessons, or please God.

———————————/—-

Author's note:

My intention behind writing this piece is to simply draw attention to the fact that animal sacrifice is unreasonable and unjustifiable.

Glossary:

Qurbani and Bali: mean sacrifice.

Eid-al-Adha: Every year during the Islamic month of Dhul Hijjah, Muslims around the world slaughter an animal and celebrate the festival of Eid-al-Adha

Shakti: Divine power or energy worshiped in the form of the consort of Shiva.

Abbu/ Abba: Father

Story 9

THE FRAGILE MIND

The café resonated with his childlike laughter. Manim looked around excitedly, his face shining bright, his nostrils flared up, inhaling the myriad aromas of freshly baked pastries and pies wafting through the kitchen backdoor, marked 'For staff only.' People looked on, amused. Strangers, who hadn't smiled in a while, buried under the weight of everyday perils and stresses, suddenly found themselves relaxing, their frowns disappearing, smiling and calmly sipping their beverages.

He couldn't remember the last time he had been so happy. He'd met Lucie a week ago for the first time right here in this café', yet it did not seem like it. Like with bosom pals, Manim found himself sharing such stories with Lucie as he hadn't talked about to anyone in a while. When in her presence, Manim's pent-up emotions erupted like some long dormant volcano becoming suddenly active.

Ekphrasis

How quickly and beautifully had their friendship blossomed. Manim chatted, at times without catching a breath in between sentences, telling Lucie all about Maxim and their twin girls, Aria and Elie, and their times together. He confided about Maxim's love for adventure.

Lucie heard about their paragliding trip while Maxim was in her first trimester of pregnancy, the story of their capsized boat while river rafting as well as their baking sessions with the girls, the hare chase, and the family barbecues ... He twisted in his seat taking out his wallet and excitedly showed off a faded photograph of the four of them. The barista stopped churning the coffee in the blender and looked on with amused interest.

Time slipped past. Manim kept no account of it, too engrossed in his newfound friend. Dusk set in. Every so often the barista would come and refill his cup of coffee dutifully. Attentively, Manim would ask Lucie if she'd like a refill too. The sea of faces around him changed from time to time as new people came in and previous diners left... Nebby spectators.

As night fell, Father Collins found Manim, sitting in a corner in the café, his jumbled thoughts tumbling out one after the other, pitching them to the empty chair opposite him. Unbeknown to him ... Alone... He addressed the demons of his past with his imaginary friend, Lucie.

Almost mechanically, Father Collins gently guided him to his feet, cajoling him out of the cafe' and taking him home. It had become a routine. The grief of having lost his wife Maxim and his two girls in an accident had been too immense to bear for Manim's fragile mind.

Story 10

THE WIN

"But where is the suffering?" Massimo asked sounding, disappointed. "What a waste!" He thought to himself. "Twenty days and as many sleepless nights. The perils of reaching such a sensitive zone. The number of palms he'd had to grease, the cost of transportation, food and accommodation to top."

Standing in the midst of overcrowded camp, refugees lying cramped next to one another, sickness and stench hanging heavily in the air, hungry howling naked infants clinging onto milk bereft breasts of malnourished mothers, swarms of houseflies buzzing around puddles of stagnant muddy waters, poor sanitary conditions with mammoth sized sewer rats waiting for death and feast, filthy men and women standing in mile-long queues waiting for their turns to get a morsel on their plates... till patience ran thin and quarrels broke out...

There was a shortage of everything: food, water, beds, clothing, medicine and doctors. Yet, Massimo couldn't find one thing he was looking for; suffering.

He was either blind or raving mad, thought Abdul to himself. He was regretting accepting his money and smuggling Massimo through treacherous routes, crossing umpteen uniformed men on the way, putting his life at stake. But the money had been good. And Allah knows how difficult it is to get by in war-stricken worlds, especially if one has a large family.

Massimo sat down on the ground, his gaze roving to find a worthy subject, leaning against the Land Cruiser that brought him here. His Nikon Z8 ready to shoot his next winning photograph.

His eye caught a half-naked teenager squabbling for a piece of bread, incessantly going after the grown-up woman, not deterred by either the abuses hurled or the stones she was pelted with.

Swift as a leopard, Massimo clicked away, aiming not to miss any action. From uniformed men to makeshift ambulances, to the sickness and strife … nothing skipped his notice or camera. Yet, he wasn't satisfied. "It's all the same. The same old kind of war with the same kind of consequences. The pictures don't inspire any new emotion. There is nothing win-worthy. It's not going to be my masterpiece to the world," were Massimo's thoughts … when a rouge missile strayed from its intended trajectory and the refugee camp was blown up in a violent dust storm. Tattered remains of human anatomies splattered like an abstract of gory colours on life-size canvas… caught by Massimo's spare camera set up on a tripod some distance away… spared by some Divine intervention.

Massimo's last masterpiece of devastation and human suffering to the world. His winning photograph!

Story 11

MANOR HOUSE ON PENNYLANE

——— The News ———

Lady Dora was in the garden when the phone rang. It was Gordon. Devastated, she called out to her husband, Drake. By four o'clock they had boarded the train to Bideford and then a ferry had brought them to Lundy Island, Devon. Lady Dora doted on the old man. After mother had left the children one night, father was everything to them.

——— The Mourning ———

The manor house was full of people today, everyone dressed in black, mourners on a casual look. But only four were really in mourning. The old man's daughter Dora, his butler, Darby, his younger son's daughter Tia and the old dog, Bethan. They mourned their loss. Silently.

Tia with Bethan in tow was visiting all rooms, hoping to catch a whiff of the old man. She remembered the last time she was here five years ago, they sat on the porch reading. His old horn rims hanging down from a chain stuck behind one ear, when he would doze off mid-sentence, his snores, the rhythmic movements of his pot belly while he slept. Young Tia loved those movements. She would naughtily try to balance small articles on his belly as it moved up and down. She remembered his hearty laughter. Lost now. Teary-eyed, Bethan and Tia left the room. It was too full of memories. They tread down the stairs and into the lounge.

The family, all freshened up, gathered in the lounge right outside the library. Reagan and Gordon lighted cigars. Gordon paused to admire the old man's collection of cigars cased in an embossed metal box, personalized with his initials, LGB. Darby brought in some wine and whiskey glasses from the bar.

Reagan poured wine for the ladies.

Filling his and Gordon's whiskey glasses, he took in a long drag before speaking up, "So how did the old man pass away?"

Reagan was the old man's younger son and Tia's father.

"Cardiac arrest, the doctor said," answered Gordon, the old man's eldest.

Dora, the old man's daughter, stifled a cry. She made a cross on her chest. Her glass of wine left untouched on the mantel.

There was a long silence. Lady Gordon got up to examine a mantelpiece.

"Dinner is served in the hall," Darby announced.

Chatting, the group made to move towards the hall.

Lady Reagan stopped by the fireside in the lounge to admire a pair of silver candlesticks. Reagan joined her. They stared at a chest of drawers kept near the lounge chair. Tia, sitting in the corner with Bethan, noticed their looks; sad.

In the dining hall, Dora tried to steer the conversation towards the old man and their life in the manor house. Lord Gordon heard her and fell silent. His thoughts meandered back to his childhood, the manor house and then to Paddy, as Lady Bott, their mother was fondly called, the hippie in the night club and the fights he would hear deep into the night... He jerked himself out of his thoughts as if wishing them to go away.

Gordon being the eldest, remembered more than Reagan or Dora. Besides, Reagan was sent away to live with Aunt Martha. Dora, refusing to leave her father, had remained with Gordon in the manor house.

Lady Gordon brought up the elephant of a conversation that everyone had on their minds but had been stalling, "How do you suppose the old man divided his assets."

"Well! I don't know. But I suppose since Tia was his favourite grandchild, he must have left us a lump sum," was Reagan's observation.

"Ah! I suppose there is no consideration for being the eldest in the family," was Lady Gordon's immediate retort.

"Then what of Dora? The man loved her."

Seething, Dora left the table. Drake followed her.

Ekphrasis

Dinner over, everyone retired to their rooms. Dora awoke to a noise. Thirsty, she got up from her bed. The breeze from the open window swayed the curtains and rattled the chandelier. She walked towards the window meaning to shut it. Gazing down, towards the backyard, she thought she saw a figure. Preening, she realised it to be the shadow cast by the old oak tree, its branches swaying in the wind. Fully awake by now and unable to go off to sleep, she decided to go downstairs.

She met Reagan, bent over the fireplace, adding sticks from a sack kept nearby.

"You couldn't sleep either?" he asked looking up at Dora.

"No, too many memories of the old man. I keep feeling he is still here, somewhere around, watching over us," Dora replied.

"No. Saw his body in the morgue while coming," Reagan said.

If Dora was surprised to hear this, she did not show it. She was used to such remarks by her two brothers and their wives by now.

She went to the library, switched on the lamp and found a book to read. A pair of horn rims kept on the table nearby kept distracting her. She picked them up lovingly. Looking at them was like peeping into a pair of lively, twinkling eyes, her father's. Fondly she felt around the rim and was soon lost in thoughts, the book left untouched. It was well past two when she made to retire. Reagan had left. She met Darby coming out with wine bottles from the cellar below.

"How have you been, Darby?"

"As well as I can be ma'am with the master gone," Darby answered.

"I understand. Tell me, how was father in his last days? Did he talk about us? Had he been keeping unwell?" Dora asked, anguish in her voice.

"Master was feeble but well ma'am. He spoke very little. Ate even less. He was in conversation with Mr. March most of the time since the last few months."

"Mr. William March? The solicitor?" enquired Lady Dora.

"Yes ma'am," answered Darby.

I wonder why, Dora whispered to no one in particular.

"There were some matters of finances ma'am and then the will as far as I could comprehend with my meagre understanding of the matter, ma'am," Darby volunteered.

"Financial issues," Lady Dora repeated.

"The estate had to be mortgaged, ma'am," was Darby's reply.

"What?" This bit came as shocking news to her.

"I must get going ma'am. Must be prepared for the luncheon tomorrow, ma'am. Mr. March would be here, I suppose ma'am?" Darby's question needed no answer and Dora digesting this new information, nodded absentmindedly, climbing the staircase to her room. Drake was already asleep.

——— The Funeral and the Will ———

Dressed in all black: hats, bonnets and bows in place, they rested the old man in the family burial chambers. Decorated in wreaths, the casket was lowered with a few neighbours, the solicitor and Dr. Scott in attendance. Conversation was limited.

After the funeral, the family returned to the manor house. The table in the hall was set up with milk, bread, baguettes, butter, eggs and sausages. There was homemade plum jam. Tia was sitting in a corner with Bethan, feeding him milk and bread. They had been inseparable.

Everyone sat down to eat. Reagan talked about a farmland he had been meaning to buy, rearing Emus for eggs and meat with his share of money from the old manor house. Lady Dora thought it crass of him to be thinking of selling the ancestral home, their only link to their roots. Lady Gordon mentioned a piece of emerald cut necklace she meant to buy with her share. Lady Reagan confessed to having her eye on a boutique. She revealed she had already talked to the owner about buying it when she heard the old man's news. Post breakfast, Reagan walked up to a black and maroon rose bud, sculpted out of 22 carat gold, embellished with tiny crystals of emeralds and rubies hung in a frame over the side slab in the hall, puffing at his cigar as he stared on. "The old man did have taste," he observed, as another frame caught his eye. A piano made of wooden sticks. Briefly, he remembered music flowing in the manor house a long time ago.

Darby announced the arrival of Mr. March, the solicitor. Reagan welcomed him in eagerly, guiding him towards the library. Gordon added wood to the fire. The room now cosy, everyone gathered around. Mr. March took in his audience. How many times had he been in a situation like this one? He mused about the frailty of human behaviour. Standing there he could almost predict the end of this meeting. And for the umpteenth time tonight, he thought about the old man, Lord Gregory Bott.

Mr. March took out a black leather folder from his briefcase and removing a pale white leaf read out loud, "I, Mr. William March, the sole legal attorney and executioner of the will of Lord Gregory Bott of Four, Pennylane Manor, Lundy Island, Devon, do hereby solemnly affirm that this is the true, only and final will drafted by me and signed by Lord Gregory Bott himself in the presence of Mr..." the cumbrous legal jargon followed. The lengthy legalities in the letter were of no interest to his audience till Mr. March reached the paragraph detailing the distribution of assets of Lord Gregory Bott of Four, Pennylane Manor. It was announced that due to some incorrect decisions taken in his life, Lord Bott was forced to mortgage the manor house. That at the time of his demise, Lord Gregory Bott was penniless came as a shock to his family, especially to his two sons, would be putting it in too mild terms.

"And in the event of his death," Mr. William March continued, "if any of his children wished to retain the manor house, they would be free to do so after paying the mortgage amount in full through Mr. William March."

The room broke out in an uproar. The fights and accusations started almost immediately. The solicitor prepared, tried to answer their questions with patience. Lady Dora only stared, thinking of how much she and Drake could come up with.

Ekphrasis

———— Nostalgia ————

The next day Lady Dora awoke to some loud noises and walking down the stairs, she saw Lord Reagan and Lady Reagan already walking out of the house. Their luggage seemed to have doubled somehow. Dora looked up at the mantel and the mantelpiece was gone. She called after her brother, "Stay for a while, Reggie. Let's discuss the mortgage. You can't give up on the one memory we have of our father."

"Stay? Stay! Stay for what Dora. Did you not hear the solicitor? There is nothing here for us. The old man is mocking us in death, even as he did when in life," Reagan answered without looking back. "It will do you and Drake well too to leave before they pick the house apart."

Lord Gordon and his wife too left by the afternoon. And then Drake said he had some errands to run.

Darby and Lady Dora sat on the porch, discussing the old man and his weird ways. His love for cigars. The smoke curls in the air that he would draw and chase asking Darby to interpret what he saw in the smoke clouds! His little game, he called it. He loved art. The best of the pieces were sadly gone, sold as Darby said to ease the functioning of the manor house. Little that remained was picked up by Lord and Lady Reagan. What they both avoided talking about was that fateful night, when Lady Bott, Paddy as she was called had disappeared, leaving her three children behind.

Freedom

Dora roamed the gardens, picking up berries and bottle gourds. Dressed in a simple frock, a scarf to cover her head and some long gloves, like in her childhood, before the fancy air of city life touched her. She found freedom. She found happiness. She would read and walk in the old woody lane behind the manor house. She found her mother's cycle in the garage and would cycle over to the burial chambers, picking up flowers on the way. It seemed she wanted to take in the very special air of the place as much as possible before it would be lost forever. She realised, with her husband and brothers gone, it was not in her means to buy back the manor house.

Discovery

It was the third night after her brothers had left that Lady Dora went down to the library. She was going through the bookshelves distractedly looking for something to read when she reached the far end of the room. Her attention was caught by a cabinet in the far corner. On the bottom of the cabinet was a single, thick, dog-eared, dusty volume like an old encyclopaedia, with moth-eaten pages. She was surprised. "How was it that she'd never noticed this one before?" She thought out loud. She picked it up. It was heavy. As tattered worn-down bits of yellow-brown paper fell, she saw a lever under where the book had been. Curious, she pulled at it. Nothing happened. She tried again; this time harder. The floor of the cabinet gave way. It was a trap door. Surprised, a little edgy, she crouched and peeped down. It was dark. She returned to the lounge for a lamp.

Lamp in hand, Dora saw a wooden staircase going down to the basement. The steps creaked spookily as she ventured down. Sinewy threads of cobwebs irritated her cheeks, and she tried to wipe those off with her hands, but they just stuck all the more. The stairs led her to a small cellar-like enclosure. The place smelled dingy. She coughed up dust. Even with the lamp, the place was dark, and she had to move the lamp around the room. In a corner, she saw a wooden chest, no more than a large locker in size. It had a heavy padlock. There was no key in sight. Deciding to bring a lever or an iron rod from the garage, she quickly climbed up. Surfacing, she breathed in the fresh air. In the garage, she found what she was looking for. As she climbed back down, her lamp traced an arc towards the left side wall. She saw an old piano, its legs broken, a few keys missing, lying in a heap against the wall. Vaguely she remembered her mother's long, artistic fingers seductively playing the keys of the piano. She walked to the chest and stuck the iron rod at an angle into the shackle of the padlock, giving it a forceful twist. She realised it wasn't going to be easy. Yet, she kept at it, twisting and forcing the lock shackle till it came loose with a clank. Lifting the cobwebby, dusty lid, Dora found sheets of old yellow, time-worn pages inside. Directing the lamp light, she recognised it as sheet music.

She could almost hear the chords and rhythms tumbling around her as she read sheet after sheet of verse. Even without a piano, it was beautiful. Her heart pounding, she turned around and tripped on something. The lamp in her hand crashed down with a bang and the last flickering light revealed something she could not have been prepared for in a million years…

A skull!

She let out a shrill scream. In pitch darkness, she collapsed.

Recovery

She was lying on the sofa in the lounge with Dr. Scott calling out her name. Dizzy, she moved her head. It hurt to move. Eyes blinking, she tried hard to focus.

"It's ok. Take it easy," Dr. Scott said.

"Where? What happened? Oh! The cellar," realisation dawned.

"Yes! you were very brave to go down, exploring on your own. But rest for now. No more excitement for the night."

The Reunion

It was Dr. Scott who told them the rest. The family had been called after more bones were discovered. Darby had heard a scream coming from the library. Then spotted the open corner cabinet, its door ajar and the trap door... He found Dora and called Dr. Scott in who led the search. Gordon was devastated. He kept saying, "I knew, the old man was no good. I knew mother couldn't have left us."

Being the eldest, he remembered Paddy's affair, the fuming old man and their constant fights till mother disappeared one night and the old man declared she'd left them for the hippie she sang and played piano with in the island pub.

The irony was, they lost their father, found their mother and gained a fortune. FBox bought the sheet music for a million pounds. Dora was not sure if she wanted to retain the manor house, now that she could afford it.

Story 12

THE RUNAWAY MARE!

As the day finally dawned, Mira, the mare proudly cantered in the paddock, both nervous and excited. She had been preparing for this day for almost a month now. So many conversations she had been a part of where her troop excitedly discussed the celebrations and now finally, she was being entrusted with the responsibility. She was elated to be the one to be picked up from the stud although there were five more mares that turned four this year.

As the clock struck four in the evening, she was led out of the paddock by Gustav, her handler, towards the stall in the stables. She was very happy with the special favours she had been receiving all week. Nice hay and water-soaked grams to eat! Her bed was made softer too nowadays! Gustav gave her a bath, scrubbing her back and belly till it glistened. He cleaned her ears, scrubbing behind them till she felt ticklish. Oh! How she loved that! He dried her clean and then brushed her long white soft mane.

Mira was a beautiful female horse with smooth sloping shoulders, deep crest, relatively small head, wide bright eyes, pointed ears, smooth skin milky white and a white soft long mane. A soft brown splash mark could be seen on her forehead reaching one eye. Her mom called this her beauty spot, and she was very proud of it. Her legs were long, and firm and her muscles gleamed with health. Her pasterns accentuated. Hooves adorned with horseshoes.

Back in the stall, Gustav covered her back with a gold thread embroidered bright red rectangular cloth decorated with small diamond-shaped glasswork. The glass glittered as light reflected and appeared like small diamonds every time Mira would move. She rather enjoyed this and moved even more, irritating Gustav who chided her childish behaviour. This she did not like, being called a child! She sulked a little but behaved herself thereon. Next, Gustav adorned her four pasterns with ghunghroos (musical bells). Oh! the sound of jingling bell music felt so exhilarating to her. Her heart soared and her breast jutted out. She wanted to dance. One look at Gustav and she thought better of it. Gustav then proceeded to adorn Mira with a glittering red bridle fixed with a crest of white feathers as a headdress. A broken slab of glass was kept against the stable wall on the floor and Mira admired herself, moving fluidly from side to side.

She was now ready to be led out.

She was made to climb up an open truck, for the wedding destination was a little far off. The band all decorated in their finery too climbed atop another truck. The procession was supposed to travel some distance to reach the bride's place and all along Mira preened herself as would a bride!

Finally, they reached common ground. Mira was helped down from the truck and led to a makeshift camp. She trotted in. A little excited and a little nervous. A group of beautifully dressed young girls greeted her, admiring her soft mane, enquiring about her name from Gustav. Mira, filled with pride, felt very important indeed. It was time for the groom to come and the girls all giggling, cracking jokes brought out a bag of soft soaked grams for Mira. Mira was overjoyed as she sniffed the soaked gram taking in its aroma, preparing to have a hearty meal. The band started playing a slow melodious song with trumpet beats interrupting the flow.

Once Mira had her fill, Gustav signalled for the groom. Mira saw a weird character funnily adorned in a loud, shiny attire with a red coloured long cloth wrapped around his neck, headdress and a veil of glistening material where the character's head should have been, walk towards her, carrying a sword in one hand, wearing some mojris (traditional footwear) in obvious discomfort. A group of rowdy looking men accompanied the character. Just then something got into the band, and they started making a great noise with out of tune loud trumpets and drums. The noise deafened Mira for some moments. She froze. A group of people talking just too loudly, almost at a fighting pitch, gathered around her. Some men hitched the weird character onto her back and another woman roughly pushed an obviously discomforted, crying child into the character's lap on Mira's back. Mira just could not take it any longer. Her hearing returned, her heart could be heard beating above the drums and trumpets, her pulse raced, her breath gathered dust from the sandy ground, and she galloped top speed.

The physics, however, as it always happens comes into play at the most unnatural of places and at the most natural of times! The law of inertia came into play and Mira galloped with the groom dressed in all his finery all but hanging onto her embroidered red cloth and the child wailing loudly catching onto the groom's stole, threatening to tie a noose around his neck. The law of gravity not wanting to lag decided to show her worth. The groom with the child still hanging around his neck struck the ground. And the momentum made sure Mira could not be spanked by Gustav seen running top speed behind his pretty runaway mare!

The scene was ironically tragic and comical at the same time! The onlookers sceptical, barely controlling their laughter. The mother of the groom, her face as red with rage as Mira's embroidered finery, cussed out loud. Her put-on sophisticated demeanour all gone for a toss. The case of a beautiful runaway mare!

www.ingramcontent.com/pod-product-compliance
Lightning Source LLC
LaVergne TN
LVHW091531070526
838199LV00001B/17